For my son, Jack

The Emperor of Absurdia
Copyright © 2006 by Chris Riddell

Printed in Belgium.
All rights reserved. No part of this book may
be used or reproduced in any manner whatsoever without
written permission except in the case of brief
quotations embodied in critical articles and reviews.
For information address HarperCollins Children's
Books, a division of HarperCollins Publishers, 1350
Avenue of the Americas, New York, NY 10019.
www.harpercollinschildrens.com

Library of Congress
Cataloging-in-Publication
Data is available.
ISBN 978-0-06-144929-1

1 2 3 4 5 6 7 8 9 10
❖
First American Edition, 2009
Originally published in Great Britain
in 2006 by Macmillan Children's Books

The Emperor of Absurdia

Chris Riddell

HarperCollins*Publishers*

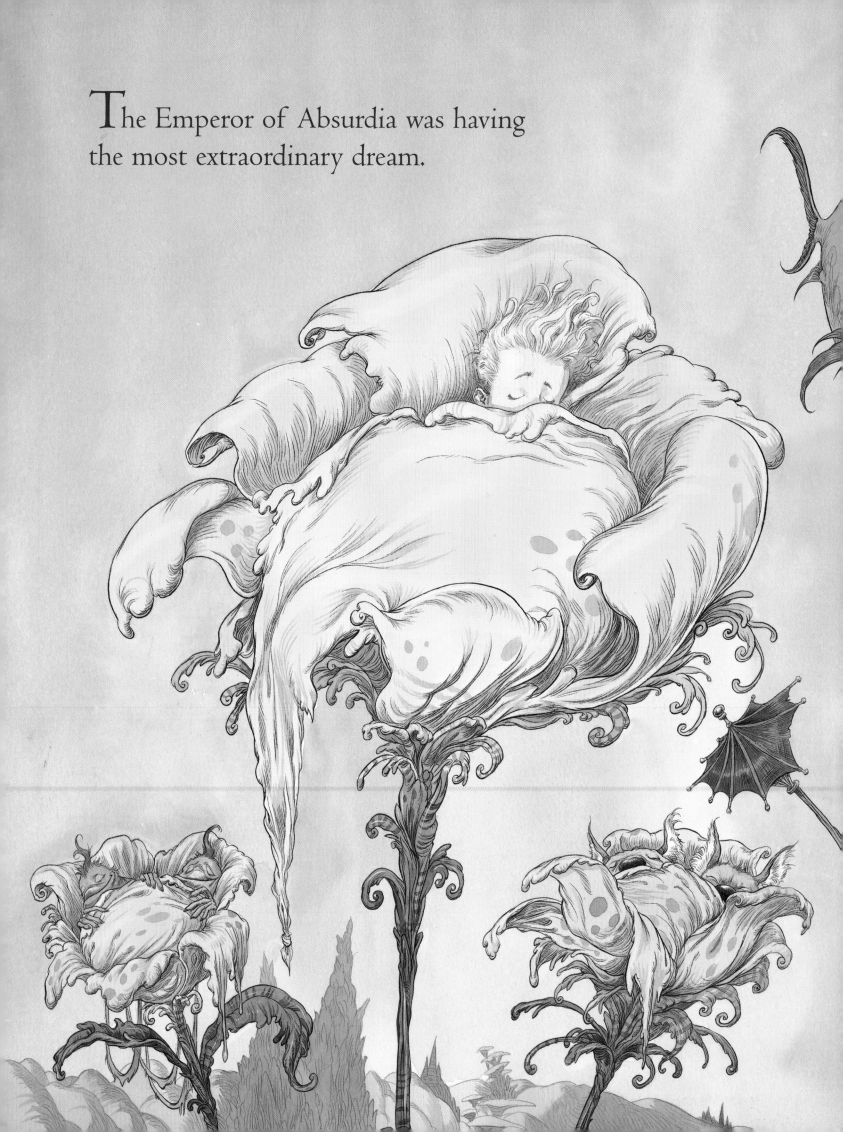

The Emperor of Absurdia was having the most extraordinary dream.

All of a **sudden** he woke to the **hoots** of the sky fish nibbling the umbrella trees.

He tumbled

out of

bed . . .

. . . into the arms of the **Wardrobe Monster.**

The Wardrobe Monster helped the Emperor get dressed—

in a woolly hat,

a crumply coat,

and a pair of jingle-jangle socks.

"Have you seen my **snuggly scarf** anywhere?" the Emperor asked.

The Wardrobe Monster shook his big hairy head.

"That's funny.
I had it yesterday,"
said the Emperor,
and he set off on a
scarf hunt . . .

. . . which took quite some time.

"It's no good," said the Emperor, sitting under a pointy tree. "I can't find my snuggly scarf anywhere."

Just then, from the top of the tree, there came a loud, pointy-sounding **squawk.**

The Emperor climbed the pointy tree and found a pointy nest . . . and there was his **snuggly** **scarf.**

The Emperor of Absurdia put on his scarf and went to his high chair.

Breakfast was served.

And then **supper**,

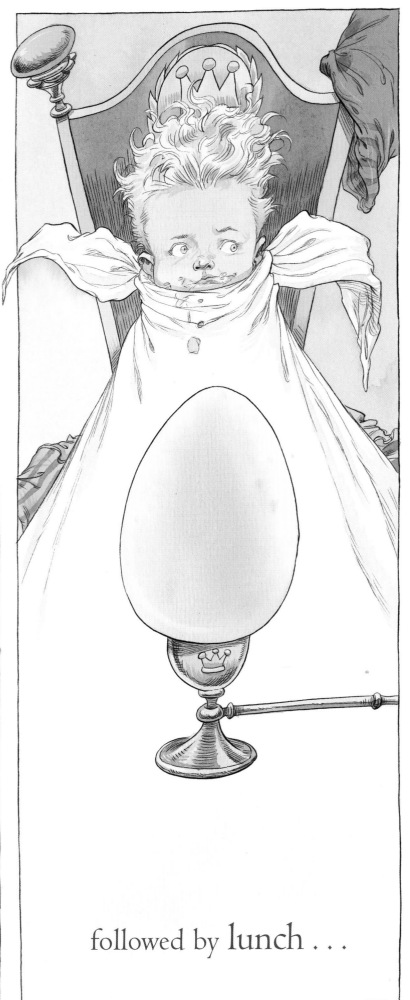

followed by lunch . . .

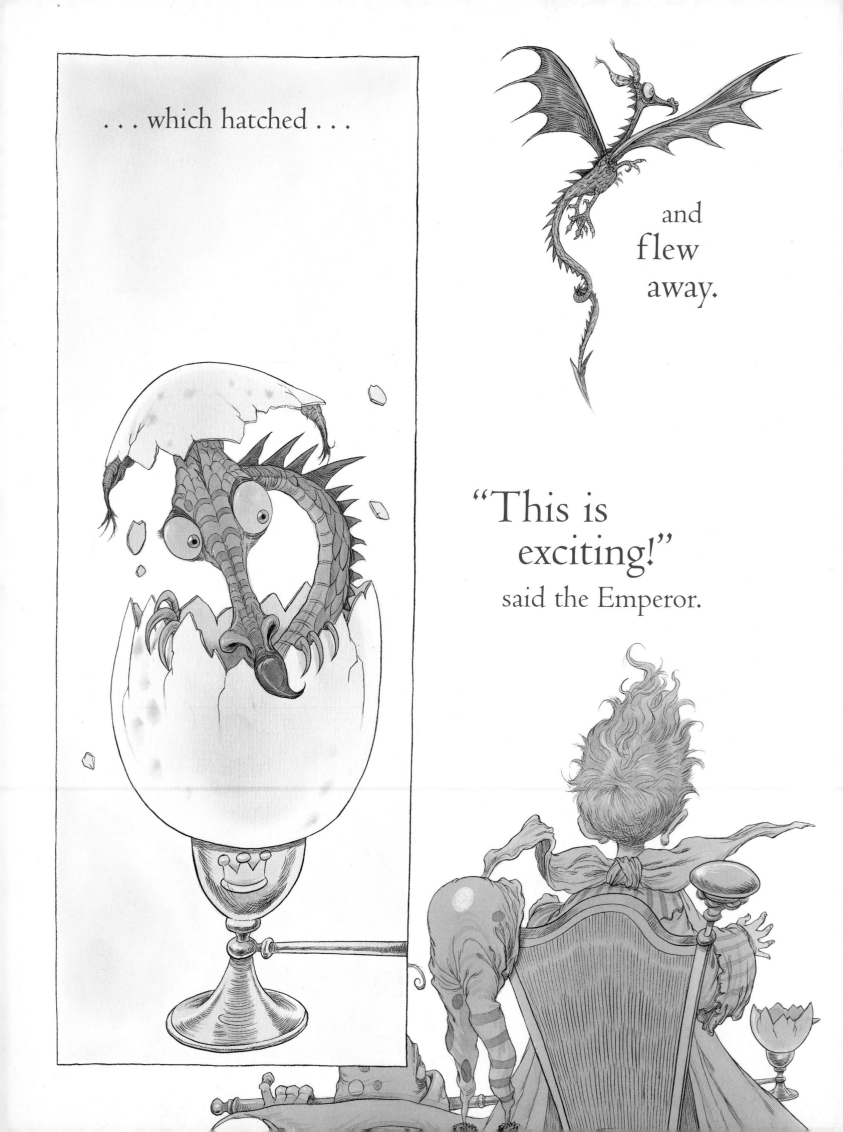

. . . which hatched . . .

and
flew
away.

"This is
exciting!"
said the Emperor.

The Emperor of Absurdia called for his
tricycle chair
and set
off on a
**dragon
hunt** ...

. . . which took quite some time.

He looked
in the
flower beds
and up the
umbrella
trees.

He looked
under
the **pillow
hills**

and over the bouncy mountains.

"It's no good," said the Emperor,
climbing down from his tricycle chair.
"I can't find the little dragon
anywhere."

He was just about
to give up when he
noticed the footprints.

They led into
a deep, dark
cave.

The Emperor took off
his woolly hat and his
jingle-jangle socks and
put them in the pocket of
his crumply coat.

Then, as quietly
as he could, he
tiptoed inside
the cave.

And
out
again!

The dragon chased the Emperor across the bouncy mountains

and through the pillow hills,

under the umbrella trees and toward the flower beds.

Then
there came a loud,
pointy-sounding
squawk
and a pointy
bird swooped
down and
caught
hold of the
Emperor's
scarf.

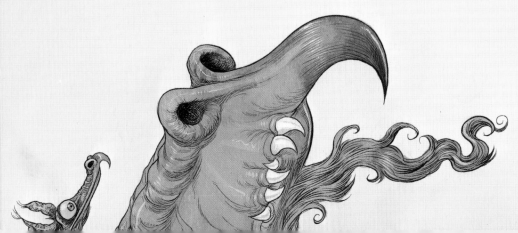

As they **flew** over the flower beds,
the Emperor let go of the scarf
and **tumbled**

down through

the air . . .

into the
arms of
the Wardrobe
Monster.

He was
so pleased to
see the Emperor
that he gave him
an **extra-
big hug**.

"I'll look
for my
snuggly scarf
tomorrow," said
the Emperor, and
the Wardrobe
Monster nodded
his big hairy head.

Then, as a big buttercup moon
rose in the sky, the Emperor of
Absurdia tumbled into bed
and fell fast asleep.

And as the sky fish snored
in the umbrella trees . . .

. . . he had
the most
extraordinary
dream.

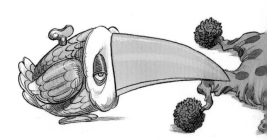